PROJECT 1

Contents

British Library Cataloguing in Publication Data

Grant, John *1930-*
    Storytime for 7 year olds.
    I. Title   II. Gordon, Mike *1948-*
823.914[J]
    ISBN 0-7214-1347-1

First edition

Published by Ladybird Books Ltd Loughborough Leicestershire UK
Ladybird Books Inc Auburn Maine 04210 USA

Printed in England (3)

Storytime
for 7 year olds

by JOHN GRANT

illustrated by
MIKE GORDON

Ladybird Books

The eight day space ship

Billy was given the *Boy's Book of Space Travel* for his birthday. He looked at the pictures of space ships, and decided to build one of his own. He told his friends Sharon, Mark and Laura, who all thought that it was a super idea. It could be their class project for school. There was to be a prize for the best one. And they just knew that a space ship was bound to win.

Their teacher, Miss Wilson, also thought it was a splendid idea. She helped to collect bottles, tubes, sticky tape, cardboard, hardboard, string and a big tube of glue. Everyone worked hard. In no time at all, it seemed, the space ship was nearly ready. It looked exactly like one of the pictures in Billy's book. It was finished off with a coat of silver paint, and up the side in big black letters was painted: *Project 1*.

"What about the rockets?" asked Mark.

"No rockets!" said Miss Wilson. "You know that you're too young to use matches!"

Billy, Sharon, Mark and Laura went to see Paddy the Junk Man. Paddy knew all about machinery. He could mend things like bicycles, and skateboards. "Paddy," they asked him, "how can we make a space ship go without rockets?"

"How about clockwork?" he said. "I've got the works from an old station clock here that might do. It's an eight day clock, but if you're planning to be away for not more than a week, it could be just what you need."

During morning lessons next day, Paddy brought the clock machinery to the school. He took the space ship into the playground and fixed the clockwork inside it. At lunch time everyone crowded round to look.

"Let's eat our lunch in there," said Laura, and she and Sharon went inside. So did Billy and Mark.

"Do you think it will really work?" asked Mark.

Billy pulled a lever marked START. The old clock clicked and whirred. Then he pushed a button marked UP. Slowly at first, and very gently, *Project 1* rose into the air.

7

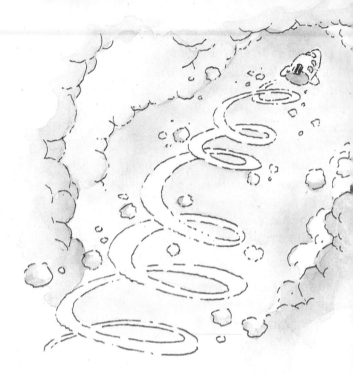

The people in the playground gasped. The space ship rose faster and faster. Soon it was only a speck in the blue sky. Then it was gone altogether!

GASP!

Billy, Sharon, Mark and Laura were too excited to eat much. That was just as well because the only food on board was their sandwiches.

They left the Earth far behind and looked
down on the moon as they whizzed past it.
Mars looked hot and dusty, so they didn't
stop there. They flew on to Saturn. It was fun

racing round and round the rings. Then, as
they were skimming the edge of the Milky
Way, Mark said, "We've been gone almost a
week. It's time we went back."

Back home, everyone was very worried indeed. But a famous astronomer came on television to say that through his giant telescope he had seen *Project 1* on its way back to Earth.

And, on a sunny afternoon, with the Town Band playing and crowds cheering, *Project 1* touched down in the school playground. It wasn't a moment too soon! The old clock struck the hour... and stopped.

And Billy, Sharon, Mark and Laura won the prize for the best project.

The cat
with
blue eyes

On fine nights the cats sat on the back fence. There were five of them, and their leader was Nelson, who only had one eye. They talked about this and that. Sometimes they had a sing-song. Anyone looking out after dark would see a row of nine green eyes.

So there was quite a stir on the back fence when a new cat arrived. All the others were black or tabby. Julius, the new cat, was a grubby white. His fur was very long and untidy. It hung down over his face, with just the tip of his nose and his ears showing. He was homeless, and Nelson made him welcome. He turned out to be a good singer. And he had a lot to talk about.

One night, Nelson had problems with some particularly troublesome mice. So, it was quite late when he arrived at the back fence to see eight green eyes in a row... and two BLUE! It was Julius. The evening breeze had blown the fur back off his face, and they all saw his eyes for the first time. None of them had ever seen BLUE eyes before!

"He's different!" cried the cats. "A troublemaker," cried Nelson. They chased Julius away from the back fence... and told him not to come back!

Julius was very unhappy. He was also hungry. He curled up in a corner of the churchyard to sleep. In the morning he went to rummage in a handy dustbin for something to eat. Suddenly a voice croaked, "Good morning. You're new around here." It was a cheeky looking jackdaw.

COOL MAN!

Julius told him his troubles. "Hang on," said the jackdaw. It flew up to its nest, which was full of the bright, shiny things that jackdaws like to steal. A moment later, the jackdaw fluttered down beside Julius with a pair of green-tinted sun glasses. Julius tried them on. "Cool, man!" croaked the jackdaw.

Julius set off that evening to join the cats on the back fence. Cats can usually see in the dark – but not if they are wearing dark glasses. Julius leapt up, missed his footing, and fell over the other side. The other cats all laughed.

Julius slunk away. It began to rain. Tired, wet and hungry, he was sitting by the roadside when a lady drove past. She stopped, picked Julius up, and took him home.

Once he was fed, dry and combed, Julius looked quite different. A neighbour looked in. "What a beautiful cat!" she cried. "He's a long-haired British white! And, those eyes! You have a champion here!"

And she was right. The kind lady entered Julius for a cat show, where he won all the prizes. He was a star! He acted on television, advertising cat food. When he made a personal appearance in the local supermarkets, the cats from the back fence went to see him. And Julius was really very nice to them. He made sure that they all got samples of the cat food he was advertising.

That night he joined them for a sing-song on the back fence. High up on his nest, the jackdaw watched and listened. He could see nine green eyes and two blue. "Cool, man!" he croaked.

Littlenose and the ants

Littlenose lived long, long ago. It was called the Ice Age. He lived in a cave with his father and mother. He had a pet mammoth called Two Eyes. One day Littlenose came into the cave carrying a huge bundle of firewood. He put it down, and said, "I've worked very hard, Father. Don't I get a reward or something?"

"Certainly not!" said Father. "Work should
be a pleasure! Look at the ants! Busy all day!
And all night! They don't ask for rewards!"
Father added.

When he had gone, Mother gave Littlenose
a big piece of honeycomb. He took it to eat
under his favourite tree. The honey was
sweet. It ran through Littlenose's fingers. It
drip, dripped on the ground as he walked to
the tree.

19

Littlenose sat under the tree. There was an ant hill close by. The ants, as always, were very busy. "I bet *they* get a reward," thought Littlenose. "From the queen ant."

It was almost bedtime. Littlenose went home. Soon, he and Father and Mother and Two Eyes were fast asleep – but others were wide awake! Like the ants. One of them had

found a drop of
Littlenose's honey.
Then another drop,
And another.

The ant signalled to
his friends. They came
scurrying, following the
trail of dripped honey.
As Littlenose slept the
ants drew nearer.
When they reached the
cave, the honey trail
ended. Perhaps there
was more inside. The
ants scurried inside to
have a look.

But there was no more honey. The ants
grew angry, and one of them bit Father. He
woke with a yell. There were ants
everywhere, biting and nipping. Father,
Mother, Littlenose and Two Eyes rushed from
the cave.

It was morning before the ants gave up
and went back to the ant hill. Father, Mother,
Littlenose and Two Eyes went back into the
cave. Afterwards, Littlenose still had to work
hard. But Father never mentioned ants. For at
least a week!

Aunt Nora's yeti

Flora McPherson's Mum was going to have a baby, and Flora hoped it would be a boy. She had wished and wished and *wished* for a brother. While Mum was in hospital having the baby, Flora went to stay with her Aunt Nora, who lived on a small farm in the country.

Flora had never been to the farm, and she was very excited. She went by train, and Aunt Nora met her at the station. Then they drove to the farm in a pony and trap.

On her first morning at the farm, Flora helped Aunt Nora to feed the hens and ducks. Then she went to look at the goats. They lived in a field with the pony, whose name was Mick. Mick also had a stable where he lived in winter.

Aunt Nora said, "There are logs to be chopped. Where's Gordon?"

Gordon came out of the stable. He was twice as tall as Aunt Nora. He was also covered with fur.

"Why, he's a yeti!" cried Flora. Gordon smiled. He had a lovely smile.

"I didn't know he was a yeti," said Aunt Nora. "But he's awfully strong. And he'll do anything for a pancake." At that, Gordon gave another lovely smile. "No, not yet," said Aunt Nora. "Not until you've chopped the logs."

Although Gordon was shy, he and Flora became good friends. She knew all about yetis – she'd read about them in books. Gordon lived by himself in a room above the stable. One wet afternoon Aunt Nora showed Flora how to make pancakes.

When they were ready, Flora took them across to the stable, and she and Gordon had tea together. Flora told him that she was going to market next day with Aunt Nora. Would he like to come too? But Gordon shook his head. Yetis don't like crowds because they are very shy indeed.

Next morning, Aunt Nora harnessed Mick to the trap, then she and Flora set off for the market. At the edge of the village, the narrow road was blocked. A truck laden with vegetables for the market had skidded and was stuck in the ditch. A crowd of men, with two horses and a tractor, were trying to pull it out.

The village policeman called to Aunt Nora,

"Won't be long, Miss McPherson. We'll have it clear in two minutes." But they didn't.

While they were waiting Flora had an idea. She jumped down and ran as fast as she could back to the farm. In the kitchen she whisked up a big bowl of batter and made a whole lot of pancakes. She put them in a tea-towel, then ran to the stable. "Gordon!" she called. "Come quickly!"

29

When he heard what Flora wanted, Gordon shook his head. But Flora showed him the pancakes and he changed his mind. He bent down and picked her up. Holding the pancakes in one hand, and clutching Gordon's fur with the other, Flora was carried like the wind across the fields to the village.

"Hello, Gordon!" said Aunt Nora in a surprised voice. Gordon put Flora down. The horses were still trying to pull the truck out. Gordon took hold of the rope. As soon as he and the horses pulled together, the truck rolled out of the ditch. Everyone cheered.

"You didn't tell me you had a yeti," said the policeman.

"Nobody ever asked me," said Aunt Nora.

"Fine chap," said the policeman. "I'd like to shake him by the hand." But Gordon had gone. He'd taken his pancakes back to the quiet of the farm.

Flora went home at the end of the week. She was sad to leave Aunt Nora and Gordon, as well as the hens, ducks, goats and Mick the pony. But she had the new baby brother she had wished for. Flora made up her mind to start wishing again. This time for a yeti... like Gordon.

The genie
of the
juke box

Kenny's dad had a café
beside a dusty side road, not
far from a canning factory. Kenny loved the
café. It had a steaming coffee urn, a little
oven, and sandwiches in a glass cover on
the counter. Best of all, there was a juke box.
It was an old fashioned one, not like the juke
box in the flashy café on the main road. The
music it played was old fashioned, too.
Kenny wasn't the only one who liked it. The
truck drivers, and the ladies from the
canning factory, liked it as well. Kenny loved

to listen to "When the Saints Go Marching In" and "Ghost Riders in the Sky" (which was scary). The tune he liked most of all was "The Teddy Bears' Picnic."

One Sunday Kenny was helping his mum with the cleaning. He polished the front of the juke box, gazing into it as he did so. Sometimes it looked like an enchanted palace.

Mum put a glass of milk and a biscuit on one of the tables for Kenny, then went outside to put some rubbish in the dustbin. As soon as the door closed behind her, Kenny looked at the buttons on the juke box and took out his pocket money. There were buttons to press for the different tunes. One button was blank. Kenny had often wondered what would happen if you pressed that one. He put in his money. Then he pressed the blank button. What would it do? There was a flash and a swoosh! A tall, thin figure seemed to leap out at him.

"Hi, kid!" said the figure. "I am the Genie of the Juke Box, come to take you into the magic Land of Music!" As he spoke, the juke box grew taller and taller, turning into a real enchanted palace. There was even a door. And the Genie led Kenny through and into the magic Land of Music.

There was music everywhere: bands
playing, people singing. A crowd of jolly
musicians marched past playing "When the
Saints Go Marching In", one of Kenny's
favourites. Kenny marched beside them,

clapping his hands to the music. Then he
followed a winding path to the top of a high
hill. Two men and two girls with cowboy hats
and guitars sang "On Top of Old Smokey."
And from farther away there came the sound
of "Somewhere Over the Rainbow."

But where
was the Genie?
Kenny thought he
had better look for
him. As he ran back
down the hill, music
seemed to come from the
clouds overhead. He looked
up, then ran even faster. The
"Ghost Riders in the Sky" swooped
down, and Kenny raced for the shelter
of some woods. A different music was
ringing through the trees. His favourite – "The
Teddy Bears' Picnic."

Kenny saw the little bears in front of him,
dancing and playing in a clearing. A clock

struck in the distance. One-two-three-four-five-SIX! And he remembered the words: "At six o'clock their Mummies and Daddies will take them home to bed...!"

And here they were. The woods seemed full of large and dangerous grown up bears as well. Kenny took a couple of steps backward. Too late – they'd seen him, and they gave chase.

Kenny turned and ran for the door in the
juke box. The bears were getting closer.
Kenny ran faster. The juke box door seemed
to be getting smaller and smaller every
minute. Just in time, he managed to squeeze
through. Rushing into the safety of the café,
he bumped the table and knocked over the
glass.

Mum came in to find Kenny sitting rubbing his eyes. "Dozy," she said. "You've been working so hard, you fell asleep. And you've spilt your milk."

Kenny felt in his pocket. His money was all there! Later, when he looked for the blank button on the juke box, it wasn't blank at all. There was the name of a tune on it – "Dreaming."